The Biggest Easter Basket Ever

By Steven Kroll

Illustrated by Jeni Bassett

Cartwheel
·B·O·O·K·S·®

SCHOLASTIC INC.

New York   Toronto   London   Auckland   Sydney   Mexico City   New Delhi   Hong Kong   Buenos Aires

For Kathleen
— S.K.

To Rebecca, Rachel, and Nathan, with love
— J.B.

Text copyright © 2008 by Steven Kroll.
Illustrations copyright © 2008 by Jeni Bassett.

All rights reserved. Published by Scholastic Inc.
SCHOLASTIC, CARTWHEEL BOOKS, and associated logos
are trademarks and/or registered trademarks of Scholastic Inc.
Library of Congress Cataloging-in-Publication data is available upon request.

ISBN-13: 978-0-545-01702-2
ISBN-10: 0-545-01702-5

10 9 8 7   11 12

Printed in the U.S.A.   40
First printing, February 2008

Once there were two mice who fell in love with the same Easter basket. But a lot had to happen before they did.

The week before Easter, moms and dads in Mouseville were spring-cleaning and baking cookies when the mayor made his announcement.

"We will have a gala Easter celebration on the village green.
We will have an egg-rolling contest and an Easter egg hunt."
   Everyone cheered, "Yippee!"
   "And whoever brings the biggest Easter basket will win a prize!"
the mayor added.

"Wow," said Penelope. "I'm going to make mine out of bark!"

"I'm going to make mine out of cattails," said James. "Everyone in Mouseville loves cattails."

"I'm going to make the biggest Easter basket ever," said Clayton, the house mouse.

"I knew you'd say that," said his friend Desmond, the field mouse. "But I'm the one who's going to make the biggest Easter basket ever."

"Oh, really?" said Clayton.

"Yes, really," said Desmond.

That night, Penelope and
James did some serious thinking.
And out in the country, Clayton
and Desmond did the same. It
was Easter vacation, so they had
no homework.

The next morning, Clayton raced
to the basement. Behind the old Christmas
wreath and the broken skis, he found what
he wanted: the big straw Easter basket
his parents had made when he was just a
baby mouse.

He pulled the basket free, pushed
it up the stairs, and placed it right in the
middle of the living room.

Over at Desmond's, there was no basket, but he and his brother, Morris, were making one out of twigs. By the end of the day, their big Easter basket sat in the middle of their living room.

"That's the biggest Easter basket I ever saw," said Desmond.

"Sure looks like it to me," said Morris.

That evening, when Clayton's family came in for dinner, Dad said, "Son, what's our old Easter basket doing in the middle of the living room?"

"It's going to be the biggest Easter basket ever," said Clayton. "It's going to win the town contest."

"But what will it have inside?" Dad asked. "That's important, too."

"I hadn't thought about that," said Clayton.

The same thing was happening at Desmond's house. When Uncle Vernon came in for dinner, his very first words were, "Desmond, what's that big basket doing in the middle of the living room?"

Desmond smiled. "It's going to be the biggest Easter basket ever. It's going to win the town contest."

"But what will it have inside?" asked Vernon. "That's important, too."

"I hadn't thought about that," said Desmond.

Over at Clayton's house, Dad took Clayton aside. "To help you find wonderful things to fill the basket," he whispered, "ask the whole family."

And over at Desmond's, Uncle Vernon did the same. "To help you find wonderful things to fill the basket," he whispered, "ask the whole family."

So Clayton did.

And Desmond did.

And this is what happened.

At Clayton's house, Mom contributed a fuzzy stuffed Easter bunny. Dad added a big bag of jelly beans and piles of plastic grass.

Brother Andy and sister Trudy appeared with a chocolate bunny, chocolate foil eggs, and a little stuffed duck that made a loud quacking noise. Carefully Clayton arranged everything in his basket.

At Desmond's house, Uncle Vernon contributed his own bags of jelly beans and plastic grass. Morris added two marshmallow bunnies, a dancing chick with a silly grin, and a big meringue egg with a mouse family inside. Cousins from across the road sent over a dozen candle eggs. Carefully Desmond arranged everything in his basket.

The next morning, Clayton rushed into town to check out the competition. Both Penelope and James had made baskets the same size as his! Clayton knew he would have to make something bigger and better.

That afternoon, Desmond realized the same thing.

Each was certain he had to have something extra special.

"Colored Easter eggs," declared Clayton.
"Colored Easter eggs," declared Desmond.
They both ran off to the market to buy the eggs and the food coloring.

Clayton bought five cartons of large eggs and blue, green, and purple dyes.
Desmond bought five cartons of large eggs and red, orange, and pink dyes.
Each staggered out the door with a huge pile of boxes.

They bumped into each other and fell down! Broken eggs landed everywhere.
Clayton wiped one off his head and laughed.
Desmond wiped one off his head and laughed.
"We should make this Easter basket together," said Clayton.
"No one said we couldn't," said Desmond.

The next day, they asked their families to be partners. Soon everyone was gathering more Easter treats.

Clayton organized the sorting and the egg coloring. Desmond and
Morris made a twig basket twice the size of their original.

In no time, they had the biggest Easter basket ever, and on Easter morning, with the egg-rolling contest already under way, they carried it to the town square.

Immediately, the mayor awarded both families the prize: a giant cheese bunny. Everyone danced around, munching and high-fiving. Then they shared the basket with the whole town.

"We did it!" said Clayton and Desmond, handing out chocolate foil eggs. "All of us, together."